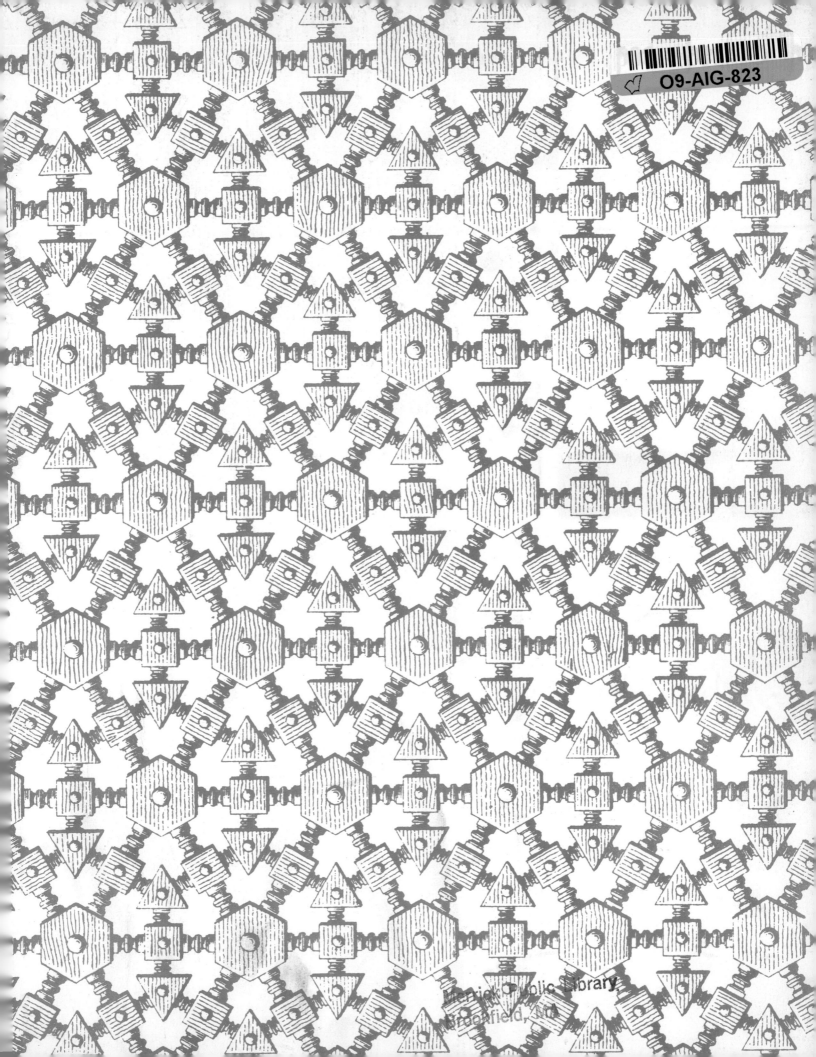

O9-AIG-823

Merrick Public Library
Brookfield, MO

Aladdin and his
Wonderful Lamp

Aladdin and his Wonderful Lamp

A Story from the Classic
'A Thousand and One Nights'
Illustrated by
Jiří Běhounek

HAMLYN
London · New York · Sydney · Toronto

Retold by Luděk Kubišta
Translated by Helen Notzl
Graphic design by Jiří Schmidt
Designed and produced by Artia
Published 1976 by
The Hamlyn Publishing Group Limited
London • New York • Sydney • Toronto
Astronaut House, Feltham, Middlesex, England
This edition © 1976 Artia
Illustrations © 1976 Jiří Běhounek
ISBN 0 600 30229 6
Printed in Czechoslovakia by Svoboda, Praha
1/05/18/51

Beyond high mountains and beyond deep rivers, far in the east, almost at the Chinese borders, there was one big and splendid city. It was the biggest and most beautiful city in all the Mohammedan empire. It was the city in the centre of which, in a huge marble palace, lived the sultan himself, the ruler of that empire. The sultan was an old and wealthy man, and he was held in high esteem by all the merchants and officials and courtiers and money-changers in his whole land and in all the lands around.

In that city also lived Aladdin. Aladdin was a young man. In fact,

964455   7.19.77 . 9.95

he was more a boy than a man. And he was poor. And he was held in esteem by no one, not in the lands around, neither in that Mohammedan empire, nor in that splendid city. In fact, not even in that god-forsaken little alley where Aladdin lived with his mother, who was a widow. They lived there together in a little earthen house, just the two of them.

The sultan was an old man and all careworn. Living in such an enormous marble palace and ruling over such a large empire and so many merchants and officials courtiers and money-changers obviously brings worries.

Aladdin was a carefree lad. From sun-up to sundown he ran through the streets with the same carefree and ragged and grimy lads. They ran barefoot, they roamed the streets and they played. They thought up all sorts of glorious adventures in faraway lands and they played all sorts of naughty pranks on people right there in the city. Now and again in the marketplace, they would even roll a melon away from the fruit-dealer's stall and around the corner they would break it and eat it. Of course, they didn't do this out of mischief alone. They also did it out of hunger. They were poor lads.

One day in the height of the summer, they ran to the little nook behind the mosque and there, all at once, they became as quiet as mice. For there they were stealing figs. Aladdin, the most nimble and the most daring of them all, climbed all the way to the top of the tree, where the figs were soft and sweet, and he gobbled them down until he had to gasp for breath. Then he threw some down to his friends, who did not dare to climb all the way up to the top.

It was shortly after noon. All the merchants and officials and courtiers and money-changers had retired to their shady rooms and there they lay down on divans to doze off for a while. The sultan lay beneath a canopy of palm leaves on the terrace of his palace and he too was trying to doze off and forget his worries. Even the soldiers at the city gates were napping. The camel-driver was also dozing. He was the

6

camel-driver who owned the fig-tree in the little nook behind the mosque. Even the camel-driver's camels were snoozing. Everyone who had finished eating lunch lay down in the shade and napped.

Only Aladdin and his friends were stealthily picking figs, and they had plenty of time for it, since everyone everywhere was sleeping.

They did not notice that not far off under a mulberry tree stood a fine horse, beautifully saddled and in the saddle on the horse sat an exquisitely dressed stranger. The stranger's complexion was dark brown. And his eyes were piercing and evil. Motionless he sat on the horse and watched the grimy youths stealing figs.

But the stranger was not at all interested in figs. He was interested only in that nimblest and most daring lad at the top of the tree, young and high-spirited as a yearling colt and as ragged as the poorest pauper in the city.

When he had finished picking figs and climbed down, the stranger whistled and summoned him with a dark finger on which shone a golden ring.

Curious, Aladdin ran to him and stared at the stranger's exquisite clothes and the gilded saddle and straps and stirrups.

'What is your name?' the stranger asked him. 'And where were you born?'

'They call me Aladdin. And where else would I be born than here in the city?'

'Would you like to enter my service, Aladdin? You will not be sorry.'

'In foreign lands, sir? And for a long time?'

'For one day and one night. And just a little distance beyond the city. And I shall pay you as if you had worked for me for seventy-seven days. Here is your money!'

And the stranger threw Aladdin a little pouch. It was full of copper coins.

'But you will do everything that I command. Do you understand?'

'I understand, sir. He who pays the piper, calls the tune. That holds true also for us in the city. I should like to take this money to my mother, may I? She will be happy.'

'You shan't go anywhere. Not until tomorrow. We shall start out right now, at once.'

And they started out. The stranger rode on his horse, Aladdin tucked the pouch inside his shirt and ran behind him. And the stranger smiled in satisfaction.

He was not an ordinary stranger. He had come all the way from Africa. And he was a powerful magician. Once long ago, he had read in magic books that somewhere in the world was a lamp and nothing on earth was more magical than that lamp. Whoever gained that lamp

would become the master of all the genies, as many as there were beneath the earth, on the face of the earth and above the earth in all the atmosphere. For many years, following this, day and night, he had poured through magic books and examined magic tablets and drawn magic figures and calculated magic numbers, until at last he had discovered the place where the lamp was hidden. He discovered that it was far from his African dwelling, beyond many mountains and many rivers, close by a large and splendid city in the Mohammedan empire, near the borders of China. The lamp was hidden there, at the foot of the mountains behind the city, under a crooked pine tree, in a rock. He smiled with satisfaction when he learned all this and, the very next day, he commanded his servants to saddle the finest horse and to prepare everything that was advisable for a long journey.

The night before his journey, he read from some more magic books and he learned that he must not go into the rock for the lamp himself. That he must send a lad who was born in that very same Mohammedan city, and it must be a lad nimble and brave, and as young as a yearling colt, and he must be the poorest pauper in the city.

He set out and he travelled for a year and a day. He found the city, he also found the base of the mountains and he even found the crooked pine tree and the rock inside which, according to his magician's calculations, was the secret hiding-place. In the little nook behind the mosque, high in the fig-tree, he then found the very young man that he needed. All that was left was to go and fetch the lamp. And to become the master of all the genies, as many as there are beneath the earth, on the face of the earth and above the earth in all the atmosphere.

It was already evening by the time they reached the foot of the mountains. The stranger rode all the way to the spot under the crooked pine tree, which grew high up on the rock. He climbed down from his horse, and he ran his magic fingers over the rock face until he found the very spot which the genies used to pass inside the rock. There were, it goes without saying, no doors. It was a smooth hard rock, without holes and without cracks. Genies, of course, can pass through walls — even walls of rock.

'Here at this very spot you will go inside, into the rock. Do you understand?' the stranger said to Aladdin.

'How on earth, sir, could I go into rock? There isn't a hole in it, not even a little crack. Even a mouse couldn't crawl in there.'

The stranger smiled and ordered Aladdin to gather a little dry brushwood. Then he set light to the brushwood and sprinkled a fistful of white powder on the flames. Fragrant smoke rose from the fire and the stranger wafted it away with a corner of his magic kaftan, whispering magic incantations all the while. Before long, a rumbling echoed from within the rock, the earth shook, and the rock cracked and opened. And in the opening a marble staircase appeared, which led down into the bowels of the earth.

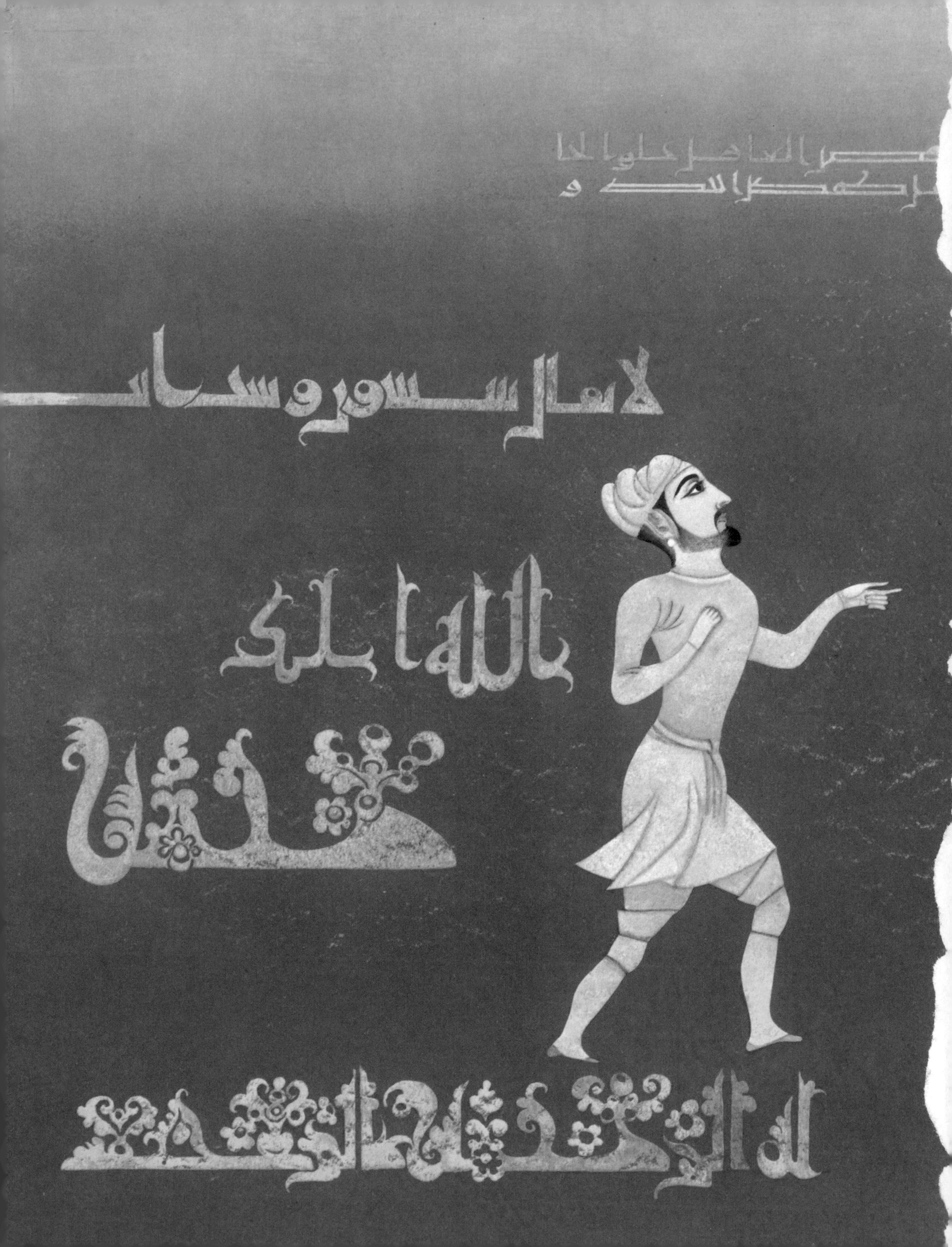

Aladdin was a daring lad, but all the same his chin began to tremble and his teeth chattered a little.

'You are a magician, sir?' he quavered.

'Silence!' the magician cut him short. 'Ask no questions. Now you will enter inside the rock. Here is some more money.'

And the stranger threw Aladdin a pouch of silver coins. Aladdin tucked it into his shirt and glanced into the opening in the rock.

'Command me, sir,' he said, boldly. 'Now I am not even the teeniest bit afraid.'

'You will climb down twelve stairs,' the magician answered. 'You will step into a large garden full of apple trees and peach trees and almond trees. Their branches will be bowed, laden with ripe fruit. And that fruit will give off a shine as radiant as the sun. But you will hurry on, until at the end of a garden you come to a little shrine covered with golden shingles. The little shrine will have an iron door, which will be locked. But you will take this ring of mine with you. When you twist it around on your finger, before you will appear the genie of this ring; he knows how to open that which is locked. He will open the iron door for you and you will step into the shrine. There you will see many costly and beautiful lamps and among them will be one lamp that is plain and ugly. Take no notice of the beautiful ones. Pick up the ugly one and bring it to me. But hurry, Aladdin. Will you do everything that I have commanded you?'

Aladdin fingered the two pouches under his shirt, glanced once more into the opening in the rocks and slipped the magic ring on his forefinger.

'And why shouldn't I do it?' he replied. 'But what is the point of all this toil and trouble for one hideous lamp?'

'Don't ask questions. Go on!' the magician demanded.

And the stranger gave Aladdin a little push, so that he ran down the twelve marble steps. He walked through the garden and found the little shrine with the locked iron door. He twisted the ring and in a flash, before him stood a genie.

'What do you desire of your slave?' the genie asked him in a terrible voice.

'Good day,' gasped Aladdin, though it was already dark night. 'Would you know how to open this door for me? It's locked and barred.'

The genie bowed and breathed on the door. It creaked open and Aladdin stepped into the shrine. There he saw a great many costly lamps and among them, one ugly one, just as the magician had said. It was still not clear to him why all this toil and trouble should be taken for one ordinary tin lamp which was, moreover, all dust-covered and rusty, but he shrugged his shoulders, took the lamp and hurried back.

As he walked back through the garden, he picked a few peaches and a few apples and stuffed them into his shirt, along with the pouches of

money. He also quickly pulled down a branch of the shining almond tree and filled his pockets full of almonds. Then he hurried out of the garden and up the marble steps.

'Hand me the lamp, Aladdin!' the stranger called out from above.

Aladdin gave him the lamp, caught his breath, and stepped up to the last step.

But it did not serve the magician's ends for Aladdin to return from inside the earth back into the world. He knew that later, at home, Aladdin might describe all that he had experienced and seen. So the magician had decided to take the lamp and then cleverly knock Aladdin back down into the cave and, with his magic arts, to neatly close the rock over him again.

And so he took the lamp from Aladdin, placed it on the ground and hurriedly sprinkled another fistful of white powder on the glowing ashes, whispering a magic incantation as he did so. A rumbling echoed inside the rock, stones began to cascade down and the marble staircase collapsed under Aladdin. The rock was closing over him.

The magician smiled and rubbed his hands together. But instantly the smile froze on his lips, for as the earth trembled, the lamp on the ground in front of the opening swayed, toppled over and tumbled down after Aladdin. And the rock closed over it and over Aladdin.

Now the magician knew from his magic books that he must not open the rock a second time and take the lamp from it. If he did, he would pay with his life. He cursed angrily, mounted his horse and rode away from the foot of the mountains, away from the Mohammedan empire and set off on the return journey back to his home in Africa.

Meanwhile Aladdin sat on a stone down in the dark cave, buried alive. It was as if the garden too had been swallowed into the earth. All that was left to Aladdin was that extinguished, hideous lamp. But suddenly Aladdin remembered the magic ring. He twisted it and instantly the genie stood before him.

'What do you desire of your slave?' he asked in a terrible voice.

'Good day,' gasped Aladdin (even though it was still night). 'I understand you can open everything that is closed.'

'Yes, I can,' the genie boasted.

'You could even open the rock?' Aladdin asked.

'Command me and I shall open it,' was the reply.

'Open it!'

The genie bowed and breathed on the stones. The rock opened and Aladdin stood up, tucked the lamp under his arm and walked out from the bowels of the earth back into the world.

'I can also fly human beings through the air, should you wish it,' the genie called out once more behind him.

'I should like that. On foot it is half a day's journey back to my home. Fly me to my mother.'

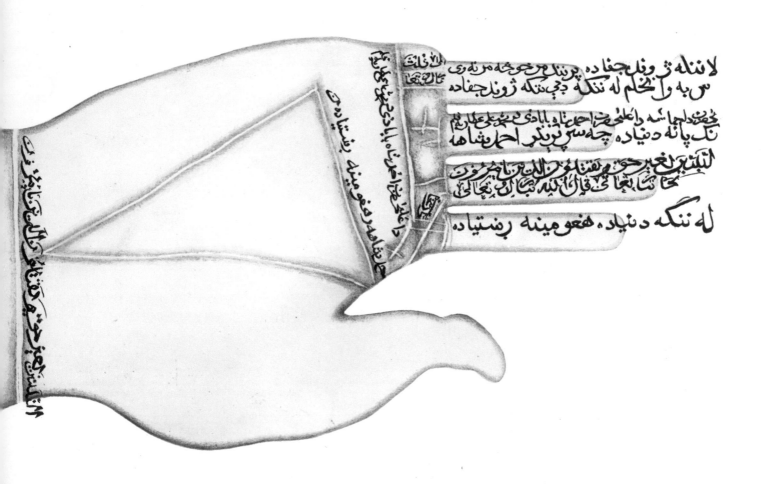

The sun had not yet risen over the eastern mountains and Aladdin was already sitting at the table at home, breakfasting on corn pancakes which he drank down with goat's milk. As he ate, he told his mother everything that had happened to him. And he gave her the pouch with the copper coins and the pouch with the silver coins. They counted the money and found they could pay the sultan's tax-collector the taxes which they owed him and they still had enough to live on for a whole year.

But the year soon went by and the money ran out. One morning Aladdin sat at home at the table and he waited for his corn pancake for breakfast. But his mother sat down beside him wringing her empty hands.

'We don't even have any cornflour left, Aladdin,' she said, sadly. 'Whatever shall we do?'

'Don't worry, mother. That old lamp which I brought last year from inside the earth must be somewhere in the attic. Take it to the junk-dealer and sell it to him and buy a bag of flour and a drop of hemp oil. Then we'll think of something else.'

The mother climbed to the attic and got the lamp from the junk-heap. Seeing how dirty it was, she thought she would take it down to the courtyard and clean it a little so the junk-dealer would pay more for it.

So she sat in the courtyard holding the lamp in her lap and began to wipe and scrub it with fine sand. Instantly a genie appeared before her.

'What do you desire of your slave?' he asked her in a terrible voice.

Aladdin's mother started in fright. She dropped the lamp in the sand and ran into the house. But Aladdin jumped forward, picked up the lamp, looked fearlessly at the genie and said to him very sternly, 'Stop scaring people. And who are you?'

'I am the lowest of the genies of the lamp. What is your command?' the genie replied.

'And what can you do?' Aladdin asked. 'We don't need to have anything opened.'

'Genies of the lamp can do everything,' said the genie. 'Command me.'

Aladdin gave a soft whistle and scratched himself behind the ear.

'For a start, bring me something for breakfast,' he said, practically.

The genie vanished but in an instant he returned again carrying a big silver platter and on the platter were twelve silver plates with slices of meat, smoked and roasted, fish and scrambled eggs, a salad of cucumbers and beans, and a selection of griddle-cakes and cocoa sponge-biscuits. To go with it, he brought a bottle of white wine and a bottle of red wine and a pot of black coffee. Then he bowed and vanished.

Aladdin called his mother and they ate and drank. When they had finished, there was still some left over!

20

'Now at last I understand it, mother,' said Aladdin. 'Now I finally know why that stranger sent me into the bowels of the earth. And why he wanted this ugly lamp and not those costly and beautiful ones. This lamp is magic. When you ran your finger over it, a genie appeared. And the genies of the lamp can do everything, you see?'

'Even if it is magic,' said his mother, 'take it away somewhere. I don't want to have such a wizardly mischief-maker in the house.'

'We'll put the lamp back in the attic,' Aladdin said to appease his mother. 'So you won't have it before your eyes. It's a shame to throw it away. And we'll only summon the genie when our situation is desperate. Do you agree?'

His mother said no more. At noon they finished eating the meat and in the evening, the griddle-cakes. The next morning Aladdin took one of those silver plates and sold it to the junk-dealer. He received a gold piece in exchange for it. A few days later he took a second plate to a different junk-dealer and got three gold pieces for it. And for the third plate, he got eight whole gold pieces.

Aladdin found he liked having wealth and finally he took all the plates that were left, even the big platter, to the junk-dealers. He earned a great many gold pieces from all those dishes and with the money he bought supplies of flour and meat and peas and lard. He bought for himself a blue kaftan, a yellow turban and sandals of calfskin and he began to strut around as if he was a lord.

That was all very well, but time passed and his money ran out. So he climbed quietly up to the attic, in order to run his fingers secretly over the lamp. He meant to summon the genie and get him to bring some more of those silver plates. But as he was rummaging through the junk-heap looking for the lamp, he found his old shirt and beneath that shirt, a pile of apples and peaches and almonds which he had brought from inside the earth at the same time as the magic lamp. He had forgotten all about them! He picked up one of the apples and saw that it wasn't an apple at all — it was a coloured and brilliant precious gem! Quickly he looked at the rest of the apples and peaches — they were all precious gems. He cracked open an almond shell, and inside it was a pearl. He took one jewel apple and one jewel peach and two pearls and hurried into the city to the junk-dealer.

But as he was walking through the city, all at once he heard a voice calling out and then he saw the sultan's crier. The crier was announcing loudly that in a little while through those streets they would carry the sultan's daughter, who had expressed a desire to look beyond the gates into the sultan's gardens. She would stop to refresh herself and to pick some flowers for a vase.

Aladdin pressed himself against the wall and in a little while, he saw a stately procession and in the procession was a litter of cypress wood, carried by slaves. Without a doubt the sultan's daughter sat in the litter. Aladdin was certain of it, even though he did not see her.

She had her curtains drawn. He only caught sight of her small hand, poking out a little from the window of the litter. A little white hand, delicate and gentle as a lily blossom.

The procession passed by and Aladdin trudged home. He forgot about the junk-dealer. He walked with his head bowed and sighed softly.

He sighed and sighed, for he had fallen in love with the sultan's daughter. And from that time on, he thought about her day and night. In his dreams and when awake, he constantly saw before him that fragile little hand, gentle as a lily blossom.

He had fallen in love, he didn't eat and he didn't sleep and nothing made him happy. But how could he think about the sultan's daughter at all, he, Aladdin, from the little earthen house? It was utter madness.

'Is something tormenting you, Aladdin?' his mother asked him,

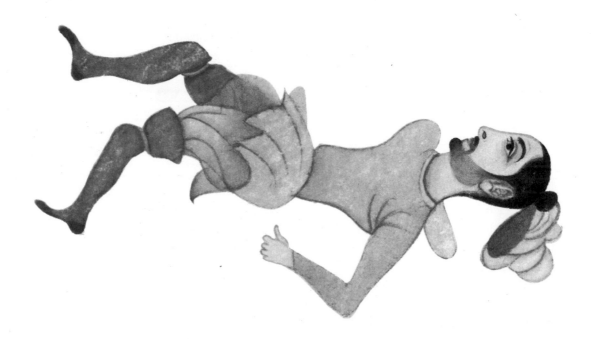

when it had already lasted many days. 'You don't look at all well. Are you feeling ill?'

'I am ill, mother,' he sighed. 'In fact, I am desperate. And there's no help for me.'

'We promised one another that when we were desperate, we would summon the genie of the lamp,' his mother said gently. 'Summon him.'

Aladdin brightened a little, thought a little, kissed his mother gratefully on the cheek and climbed up to the attic. There he ran his fingers over the lamp, and at once the genie stood before him.

'What do you desire of your slave?' he asked in a terrible voice.

'I want to see the sultan's daughter,' said Aladdin. 'Can you arrange it?'

'I can carry out even harder tasks. I am the higher genie of the lamp,' replied the genie.

25

'Stop boasting and don't waste time,' snapped Aladdin. 'Make me invisible and fly me through the air to her chambers.'

The genie blew into the air and before Aladdin knew what was happening, he was already standing in the centre of an ornate and perfumed chamber. And there, right in front of him, half-sitting and half reclining on a flowered divan, the sultan's daughter, Badrulbadura was gazing at herself in a little oval mirror and slave girls were combing her hair with a tortoise-shell comb.

Aladdin held his breath so he would not give himself away and he stood, rooted to the spot, until the lovely Badrulbadura touched the velvet soles of her feet on the sheepskin fur in front of the divan. When a pair of embroidered slippers had been slipped onto her feet, she pattered away into the next chamber.

After that, Aladdin strode home and sighed even more despondently. And at home he just sat at the table not wanting to eat or sleep or do anything.

'Have you fallen in love, Aladdin?' his mother asked him. There's no other way I can explain your torment to myself.'

'I have fallen in love, mother,' he replied, simply. 'Whatever shall I do now?'

'Why, the answer is simple,' said his mother. 'Tell her about it, and her parents, too, that you wish to take her for your wife.'

'I was just thinking about that, mother. I beg you, go and see her father and ask him to give her to me as my wife,' said Aladdin.

'Yes, of course I'll go,' said his mother. 'Don't be afraid, I shall arrange everything. And who is her father?'

'The sultan, mother.'

Aladdin's mother began to lament and to dissuade him from this madness, but Aladdin won her over in the end. And he gave her a gift for the sultan to take along with her — all the apples and all the peaches which he had in the attic and which were really precious gems.

Her mother dressed herself in her very best clothes and arranged the precious gems in a wicker bowl and set off to the sultan's palace.

She waited there in the hall. She waited for a long time. Not until all the visitors had taken their turns did the sultan send his vizier for her. The vizier ushered the mother to the sultan and the sultan, after a brief look, reckoned that the woman had probably come to beg for alms.

'Speak, woman,' he commanded her. 'Beg. But briefly. I am tired and I have worries. A sultan's worries are serious worries. What have you come to beg for?'

'For the hand of your daughter, most gracious sultan. For my son Aladdin,' replied the mother.

The vizier burst out laughing. He had been thinking about the

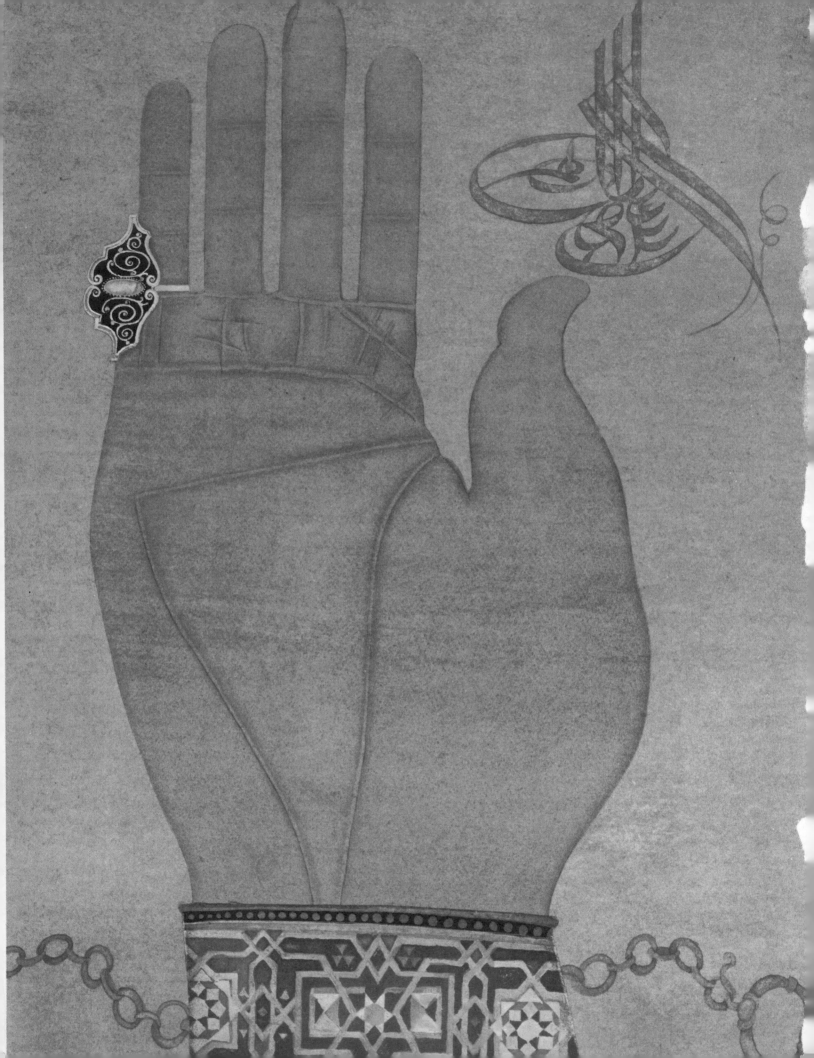

sultan's daughter for a long time himself, thinking that he would marry her so he could become sultan. He laughed at that foolish woman until tears ran from his eyes.

And finally the sultan, too, burst out laughing. Despite his being so tired and having such worries. He laughed so hard that he clutched at his belly.

The mother said not a word, but only handed the sultan the wicker bowl.

'My son sends you this gift, most mighty sultan,' she said.

'Apples?' the sultan turned up his nose.

And he took an apple, and the vizier sidled forward and took an apple too. Both of them were just about to bite into them, when they suddenly realized that they were not apples, but precious gems so costly that no prince in all the empire had costlier ones. Why, not even the vizier had such costly gems, although he was the sultan's highest adviser and minister.

The sultan rubbed his nose, surprised and a little confused.

'I see, woman, that I was seriously bit mistaken,' he said. 'Why, maybe even the emperor of China doesn't have such precious gems. What is your counsel, vizier?' and he turned to his advisor.

'Do not be hasty, most venerable one,' the vizier said, slyly. 'Let that Aladdin come tomorrow morning and bring an even better gift, if he dares to think about becoming the sultan's son-in-law. Let him give you forty platters and on them forty times as many precious gems as he sent today. And have the platters brought by forty black slaves and forty white slaves. If he cannot accomplish this, then let him drop from his mind a marriage with your daughter. Is that not clever advice?'

'That is clever advice,' admitted the sultan, who hadn't a good suggestion of his own. 'Let him come and what is more, let him also bring forty yellow slaves. Otherwise he can stay at home. Deliver the message to him, woman. And now go.'

30

'Is it bad, mother?' asked Aladdin when his mother came home highly distressed.

'It is bad, my son,' she said. 'Do not rush into misfortune. Think it all over once again. While there's still time.'

And she told him how she had fared and what the sultan desired as gifts.

But Aladdin gained nothing in thinking it over once again. He brought the lamp down from the attic and summoned the highest of its genies and gave him orders.

And the next day in the morning, from the little earthen house to the sultan's palace, a magnificent procession wended its way through the city. At its head, on a resplendent jet-black horse, rode Aladdin, dressed in clothes of silk and brocade; on every finger he had a ring and on his left-hand little finger, two rings. Then behind Aladdin walked

black and yellow and white slaves in brightly coloured robes and there were three times forty of those slaves and each one carried on his head a wrought platter and in it so many precious gems, that all the kings and emperors of the world could not put together such riches.

The procession came to a halt in the sultan's courtyard and the slaves spread the platters out around the fountain. And the sultan looked down from his balcony and clasped his hands together. Then he ran down into the courtyard and his eyes could not get their fill of all that splendour.

The vizier had to admit that Aladdin had fulfilled the conditions and so he had the right to become the sultan's son-in-law.

When the sultan grew weary of the precious gems, he turned and examined Aladdin, and saw that he was a young man with a pleasant face and a dashing figure. That in short, he would be a bridegroom as

if made-to-measure for the comely Badrulbadura. Especially when his coffers were apparently full to the brim.

'Embrace me, my son,' he said to Aladdin. 'I shall give you my daughter as your bride. Come, you must show yourself to her.'

And he took him by the arm and led him to his daughter's chambers and showed him to her.

'This is your bridegroom, little daughter,' the sultan said. 'Do you like him?'

Badrulbadura took a liking to Aladdin at first sight. But because she was well brought up and also quite proud, she did not let him see it at once.

'What have you brought me?' she asked Aladdin.

'I have brought you a gift of love,' replied Aladdin. And he drew from his bosom a necklace of pearls, as large and gleaming and as opaque as almonds. These too he had gathered from the almond tree when he was in the bowels of the earth. In each shell, though, instead of an almond, there had been a pearl. And the day before he had taken the pearls to a goldsmith and had them made into a necklace so long, that it had to be wound about the throat seven times.

The comely Badrulbadura could contain herself no longer. She allowed Aladdin to wind the necklace seven times around her snow-white throat and then she fell into his arms.

'I like him very much, father,' she whispered at the same time over her shoulder to the sultan.

Then there was a wedding, with a feast. The wedding cake was so big that they had to make the doors in the palace larger. Otherwise the cake would not have gone through them!

'You will live with me in the palace,' said the sultan to Aladdin between the courses. 'Badrulbadura would probably not like your little earthen house very much.'

And he looked at Aladdin in mockery. And Aladdin, who had

already drunk one drop of wine more than is wise, banged his fist on the table.

'We shall live in my palace!' he cried.

'I know,' said the sultan. 'You are rich and you will build yourself a palace. But that will be sometime next year. It takes a long time to build a palace.'

'Tomorrow morning at the rising of the sun, my palace will be standing,' Aladdin pounded his fist on the table once again. 'And it will be bigger than yours, sultan. Shall we wager?'

'Yes, we'll wager!' the sultan was provoked. 'And what are the stakes?'

'Your empire, sultan!'

'Fair enough,' cried the sultan. (He, too, had drunk a mite more than is healthy) . . . 'And if you lose?'

'If I lose, I shall return home. And I shall go barefoot again.'

Aladdin's mother, who was sitting modestly at the corner of the wedding table, wrung her hands and begged Aladdin to stop this

madness of his once and for all, while there was still time. But Aladdin did not relent. He rose from the table, ran hurriedly home and climbed to the attic. Then he kneeled before the lamp and ran his fingers over it. The genie promptly appeared.

'What do you desire of your slave?' he asked in a terrible voice.

'I need a palace. It must stand across from the sultan's palace. And it must be three times more splendid. Can you build it?'

'I am the highest genie of the lamp,' boasted the genie. 'I have already built a thousand palaces.'

'But I need it by tomorrow morning!' said Aladdin, desperately. 'At the rising of the sun!'

The genie winced and scratched himself a little on the stomach.

'That's impossible,' he said. 'It would be damp. The mortar will not dry that quickly.'

'But I made a wager!' Aladdin moaned. 'For the whole empire!'

'Surely you don't wish to be sultan, Aladdin?' the genie asked.

'Of course I do!' snapped Aladdin.

'That is not wise, Aladdin,' declared the genie, who was already old and had experienced and understood many things. 'Wish for something better.'

'Hold your tongue and do as I have commanded you!' Aladdin shouted at him.

'As you wish,' sighed the genie and vanished.

When Aladdin returned to the sultan's palace, the feast was still in progress. Everyone was sleepy by then, but they were all waiting to see how the wager would turn out.

And see it they did. The sun had scarcely risen when Aladdin leant from the window. With a great sigh of relief he exulted in what he saw. Quickly he invited the sultan and all the guests out onto the balcony. Across from them, on the other end of the square, stood a new palace twice as big as the sultan's palace. It shone with ornate cornices and

polished pillars and it had roofs of gold metal and before it stood servants in two rows and on the high towers fluttered flags.

'You have won, Aladdin,' the sultan admitted. 'I shall hand over control of the empire to you.'

'Not until later, sultan father,' replied Aladdin. 'Now, first of all, I shall move into my palace. In the meantime, you rule for me.'

And he took the lovely Badrulbadura in his arms and carried her across the square into his estate. The palace smelled a little of damp mortar, but Badrulbadura was dreadfully sleepy by then and didn't notice it at all.

And they lived there together happily and merrily. The old sultan still ruled and tormented himself with worries while Aladdin and his wife devoted themselves to merry-making.

Aladdin moved the magic lamp into his palace. He placed it on

a little shelf in his chamber, but he did not disclose to Badrulbadura that it was a magic lamp.

One day in the autumn, Aladdin rode out with his cortege into the forest to hunt. He planned to remain there for several days. Badrulbadura stayed at home, sitting on a divan and slave-girls played on lutes for her and sang her songs of love.

All of a sudden Badrulbadura heard a voice calling out from down in the square. She leant from the window and saw a crowd of people around a little old man. As she was curious, she sent a slave-girl to see what was happening there.

'An old man is trading lamps,' the slave-girl told her when she returned. 'He must be some sort of madman. He is giving new lamps for old.'

'New lamps for old? I don't believe it,' retorted Badrulbadura.

'Find out for yourself, mistress!' the slave-girl defended herself. 'Do you want to? I shall take that ugly rusty lamp which is standing on the shelf in the master's bedroom and in place of it I shall bring you a new one.'

Badrulbadura nodded and the slave-girl snatched the old lamp from the master's bedroom, to take down to the little old man. Soon she returned, bringing with her, a brand new lamp.

'My husband will certainly be pleased,' Badrulbadura praised the slave-girl.

The old man tucked the lamp under his cloak, smiled, and walked hastily away from the square. No one ever saw him in the city again.

He was not an ordinary little old man. He was the African magician in disguise. From magic tablets and from various magic signs, he had learned that Aladdin had escaped from the rock and that he had taken the lamp away too. And that he was alive and well and that the genies of the lamp were serving him. He had almost exploded with rage and immediately had set off to the Mohammedan empire on the borders of China. He made up his mind to take Aladdin's lamp away from him with some cunning trick.

Now he had succeeded. With Aladdin's lamp under his cloak he walked hurriedly away from the city. Once outside its boundaries, he threw off his disguise and waited for night to fall. Then he ran his fingers over the lamp. The genie appeared, ready to serve his new master and the magician demanded to be flown back to Africa without delay. At the same time he commanded that Aladdin's palace with everything in it, including the comely Badrulbadura, must also be taken to Africa.

The genie bowed and in an instant the palace with Badrulbadura in it and with the magician too, was already ascending into the air. All was flown over mountains and over rivers and over oceans and landed finally in Africa, in the meadow behind the magician's dwelling.

When Aladdin returned, he was not pleased by what he saw.

'Where is my palace? And my comely Badrulbadura?' he cried out in despair.

'During the night the palace rose into the air and flew away, Aladdin,' said the awe-struck water-bearers, who were sleeping in the square under the open sky.

Aladdin hung his head and walked wherever his legs carried him. He walked out of the city and wandered aimlessly through the country-side. He was fortunate that the sultan's guards did not find him. For when the sultan learned about the disappearance of his daughter, he flew into a rage which was aimed at Aladdin and, on the vizier's advice, he had sent the guards out to find him and to cut off his head.

Aladdin wandered through the forests and over the steppes and in the day he confided his grief in the birds, at night in the stars above. But neither the birds, nor even the stars could reveal to him where the lovely Badrulbadura was.

Until one evening, he was sitting on the grass at the edge of the woods, and in vain he pondered what he was to do. And as he pondered, and as he sighed, in his absorption he twisted the magic ring which had once helped him out of the rock and which, since that time, he had always worn on his forefinger. Instantly the genie of the ring stood before him.

'My dear genie,' Aladdin rejoiced. 'Save me just once more! Return my Badrulbadura to me! I don't know where she has gone!'

'The African magician carried her away,' the genie replied. 'And the palace as well.'

'Return it all to me, dear genie!' pleaded Aladdin.

'That is not within my power, Aladdin. Only the genies of the lamp could do that,' said the genie of the ring.

'And where is the lamp? Also in Africa? Fly me then, to Africa, genie!' cried Aladdin.

The genie bowed and in a twinkling Aladdin stood in the meadow

behind the dwelling of the African magician and before him the towers of his palace were silhouetted against the night sky.

In the palace all were asleep. In only one window did a light shine.

'That is surely the window of my lovely Badrulbadura,' Aladdin said to himself. 'She is not sleeping and is thinking of me. She is waiting day and night for me to rescue her.'

And because he was still nimble and daring, he scrambled up the pillars and cornices all the way to that window and he climbed into her room.

'Where is the lamp?' he asked, after he had greeted Badrulbadura, embraced her and kissed her.

'That hideous and rusty one?' Badrulbadura guessed. 'The magician has it with him. He never lets it out his sight. I don't understand what is so special about it.'

And Aladdin told Badrulbadura what was so special about the lamp. All night long, they planned and plotted until they finally agreed that the next day after breakfast, Badrulbadura would lure the magician out into the garden. Then Aladdin would steal into his room and take possession of the lamp.

The next day after breakfast, Badrulbadura said to the magician, 'Come into the garden with me, my lord, and let us walk there together. Will you come? I shall wait for you under the pear tree.'

'I shall come, my beauty,' replied the magician, all love-sick. For up until then he had been pleading with Badrulbadura in vain to be more kindly towards him and for her to take him for her husband.

Badrulbadura glided out into the garden and sat under the pear tree. And in a little while the magician went hurrying out after her. He was perfumed and he went as fast as his old legs would carry him. But he had not left the lamp in his room. He carried it with him.

'Here I am, my Beauty,' declared the magician, all out of breath. 'Will you be more kindly towards me? I shall fulfil your every desire!'

46

'Every one?' said the clever Badrulbadura. 'Then pick a pear for me!'

The magician stood on his tiptoes and reached for a pear.

'Not that one,' Badrulbadura reproached him. 'That one's still green. Up there, see, there are the yellowest ones. I should like one of those.'

'There's no ladder here,' the magician protested.

'You couldn't climb a tree, sir?' she asked, innocently. 'After all, you must be nimble if you wish to take me for your wife!'

The magician swore under his breath and began to scratch at the tree. But with the lamp in his hands, he simply couldn't begin to climb it. And so he laid it in the grass.

'Will you watch over the lamp for me, my Beauty?' he asked.

'Yes, I'll watch over it. I shan't move from it, you may be assured,' she said.

48

And Badrulbadura waited until the magician had climbed up into the tree. Then she snatched the lamp and scurried as quickly as she could after Aladdin.

Aladdin gave Badrulbadura a quick kiss, ran his fingers over the lamp and in a twinkling the genie of the lamp appeared.

'Hurry, genie,' Aladdin said to him impatiently, 'fly us home quickly. And with the palace too.'

The genie bowed just a tiny bit, so as not to waste time, and already everything was rising into the air — Aladdin, Badrulbadura and the palace with everything in it.

Down below the magician was just climbing down from the tree. In his hand he held a pear, and in a rage he gazed into the heavens watching his fortune growing smaller until it disappeared over the horizon. Furiously, he bit into the pear and in his rage he did not notice

49

that on it sat a wasp. The wasp stung him on the tongue, and the tongue of that evil magician swelled up so much that in the end he couldn't even breathe. He choked and he choked, right there under the pear tree.

But Aladdin and Badrulbadura were no longer there to see it. They were sitting at home on the divan and in the kitchen, tea was being prepared for them, to refresh them after their long journey.

In the meantime the sultan was waiting for his guards to find Aladdin and cut off his head. He worried so much that he fell ill and died.

So Aladdin no longer had anyone who would rule for him. And he had to become sultan. After all, he himself had wished it at one time. So he began to rule, but he found that ruling over such a large empire

and so many citizens and courtiers brought many worries. And Aladdin worried, just as the sultan had before him and he grew old and became all careworn.

One summer afternoon, all who could went off into their rooms to take a nap. Even sultan Aladdin lay on the terrace of his palace and tried to fall asleep and forget his worries. But sleep would not come to him. He had far too much to worry about — lofty, sultan's worries.

And then something suddenly occurred to him. He summoned a slave and had the lamp brought to him. He ran his fingers over it and the genie appeared.

'I am growing old and I am tired, genie,' he said to him. 'And I am tormented by worries. I don't even have time any more for my comely Badrulbadura. Being sultan is no great fun, genie. Couldn't I go back to my earthen little house? And live there with my mother? Maybe Badrulbadura would also let herself be convinced. Being a sultan's wife is not much fun either. We would go barefoot. And we'd steal figs. That is merrier, genie. Arrange it!'

The genie bowed and vanished, but in a little while he appeared once again.

'It's not possible,' he said. 'My service with you has come to an end just now. Time has run out.'

'You're not going to serve me any more?' asked Aladdin in surprise. 'But why?'

'Because you already have everything,' the genie replied. 'You are already the most powerful and the most wealthy and the happiest person in the world.'

'But I want to go back!' Aladdin lamented.

'You cannot go back. No one is ever allowed to go back,' the genie whispered and disappeared.

And along with the genie, the lamp vanished too. It was as if it had been swallowed into the earth.

And Aladdin lay and he thought and thought, until at last he realized that earlier the genie had spoken two truths and one lie.

For by now Aladdin was indeed the most powerful and the most wealthy person in the world. But he was not the happiest. Now he was less and less happy all the time.

He lay and he could not fall asleep. And in the city everything dozed. Even the camel-driver's camels stretched out in the shade of the city walls and slept.

Only a little distance away, some ragged and carefree and merry lads were stealthily climbing among the branches of a fig tree and they were gobbling down soft, sweet figs until they had to gasp for breath. If sultan Aladdin could have seen them, he surely would have envied them.

DISCARDED

398.2
JS935

Stuart, Marie

Aladdin and his wonderful
lamp

DATE DUE			
MR 3 '79			
JY 14'79			
AG 2 '79			
OC 25'79			
MY 8 '80			
JY 12'80			
MR 30'81			

Merrick Public Library
Brookfield, MA

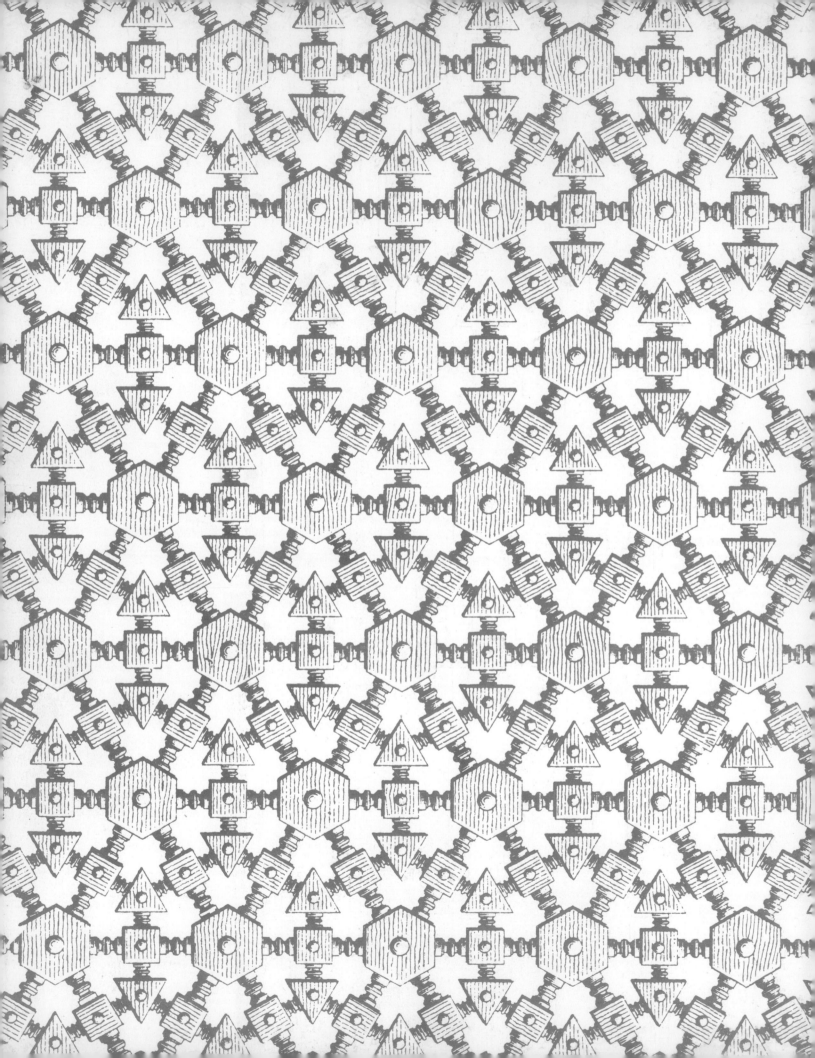